GUNFIGHTER: MORGAN DEERFIELD

HITMAN WITH A GRUDGE

A WESTERN ADVENTURE

JOHN D. FIE JR.

Previous Praise For John D. Fie Jr. From

Robert Hanlon

It gives me immense pleasure to write an opening note for this new Western from John D. Fie, Jr. Not only does Fie happen to be one of the finest writers in America today—he also happens to be one of the great campfire storytellers. Spending time with Fie... is always a pleasure and I believe you will love this new story from him... as much as I do!

Robert Hanlon – bestselling western author of "Stranger Arrives," "Timber: United States Marshal" and many others.

Previous Praise For John D. Fie, Jr From

Mark Baugher

If you like Western novels, then I'm betting you daydream about owning a vast and beautiful ranch. That is what this family owned. Big Ben was a mountain man who got there first and claimed it for himself. His wife, Ma, and he fought for every inch of this ranch and raised three children while doing it. There is an old saying: "Those that get there firstis get the mostis," and that is what Big Ben did. What a great adventure. I like this book. If you are a Western novel reader, this will be a fun read for you.

Mark Baugher – Bestselling author of "C-Bar" and several others

Previous Praise For John D. Fie, Jr From

M. Allen

This new one from John D. Fie, Jr. brings out the best in the modern Western. Not only is Fie a master of suspense and storytelling—he's also one of the most action-heavy Western writers of today. I was lucky enough to have been given the chance to read "Guns Along the Weary River" before it was officially released. What a fantastic story! I was gripped from the start and spent much of my Christmas wondering if I could write something to match his eloquent and dashing style. If you love Westerns, you will love this new one... Give it a try!

M. Allen – Bestselling author of "The Rifleman" and several others

A NOTE FROM THE AUTHOR

Howdy, friends. This is a great big thank you to all you great Western fans out there for making this new Western series, the Morgan Deerfield Saga, such a big success. I'm looking forward to bringing you even more Western action as this series continues. But I also want you to know that although this is a fictional series, I like to add just a touch of realism to the stories.

It's fun to pick out a topic and then create a story around it, and it is also thrilling to see that you like it. I hope you enjoy book two, Turbulent Times. Thank you Western fans!

DEDICATION

This book I dedicate to a die-hard Western genre lover.

A true fan who has been with me through it all,
Miss Martha Catoe Peebles!

THIS IS FOR YOU, MISS MARTHA

CHAPTER 1

Morgan and Betty sat silently by the fire after a hearty supper, enjoying the warmth. Although it was almost the end of March, the weather still hung on to those chilly winds, and sitting on the porch to watch the sunset wasn't very comfortable.

Betty looked at Morgan and could see he looked worn out and needed some rest. She suggested they spend the next day alone together. That way, they could both relax.

"Yes, Betty," he said, "why don't we. I'll let Cory know what chores need doing tomorrow morning. If it's a beautiful day, why don't we get off the ranch and go for a ride—just the two of us."

Betty smiled. Excitedly, she said, "Yes! We can take along a blanket and a picnic basket and sit somewhere and just rest for a few hours."

Morgan nodded. "That's settled then." He got up from his chair. "I'm going up, my dear. Are you joining me?"

She stood up and Morgan quickly grabbed her, holding her in his arms. He looked down and kissed her.

Betty had her arms around Morgan's neck. "Why do I love you so much, you big galoot?"

"I have no answer for that, Betty. All I know is, I'm one fortunate man to have you and Tim in my life now."

Betty smiled. "Tim and I are the fortunate ones, Morgan. I'm forever grateful to Seth for bringing us all together."

Walking upstairs, they reached their bedroom doors and said goodnight.

Morgan was having another restless night. Memories came flooding back as he tossed and turned. He finally gave up on sleep, put on his britches, then made his way downstairs to the kitchen. Marlene wouldn't be up for another couple hours.

He grabbed the coffee pot and gave it a shake. *I'm in luck. The pot's almost full.* Morgan opened the door to the stove, looked inside and saw the embers were still glowing. He stoked them, then grabbed a fresh log off the top of the woodpile sitting by the side of the stove.

Walking into the sitting room, he sat down by the fireplace, watching the small fire that was still burning. He soon dozed off, and was startled awake by Marlene.

"Mr. Morgan, are you all right?" she asked.

Still half dazed, he looked up at her. "Yes, Marlene. I just fell back to sleep. I came down to get a cup of coffee."

Marlene looked concerned. "Why don't you go upstairs and get some better rest in your bed, Mr. Morgan?"

"I think I'll have a cup of coffee first. Is it time for breakfast already?"

Marlene gave a soft laugh. "Mercy, no. I heard someone snoring and came out to see who it was. Are you sure you're all right?"

"Yes, Marlene. I'm fine. I just miss sitting in front of a fire now and then."

Marlene wasn't sure if she believed him and made up her mind to talk about it later with Miss Betty.

Morgan must have read her thoughts. "Marlene, there's no need to let Betty know I was sleeping down here again, okay?"

Marlene hesitated. "I can't promise you that, Mr. Morgan. I'm sorry. But if the subject doesn't come up, I won't bring it up. How's that sound?"

"Sounds like a deal to me. I shouldn't have asked you in the first place. I apologize."

"Let me get you that cup of coffee, Mr. Morgan. Then promise me you'll get some more sleep in your bed."

"Okay. I promise."

Marlene went into the kitchen and returned with his coffee. "Remember, Mr. Morgan. You promised."

So this is what it's like having women around! He chuckled.

Morgan sat in his chair thinking about how he was now in charge of three cattle ranches—the Broken Branch, the N Bar H, and the Trails End.

The price of beef was down. It had been a hot topic of discussion at the cattlemen's conference Morgan and Betty had attended in the territory's capital a couple weeks ago.

A lot of the cattlemen were going ahead with their cattle drives, while others had decided to hold back. Morgan had made the decision to hold back and cull the herds, then send them all down to the beef buyer in Summit. Suddenly a thought came back to him—the stranger at the conference who kept staring at him.

Morgan knew that face and the look the man had given him—he recognized Morgan. As he took his last sip of coffee, the man's name came back to him—Duke Holcomb! *The Holcomb brothers—they dogged my trail for months after I killed their brother.* Morgan shook his head. *I told Betty I didn't want to go to that conference.*

He assured himself that when the time came, at least he would know who was coming for him, and he also knew how they operated. They were backshooters, all of them. Morgan looked at his guns hanging on the wall.

No! I'm not putting on those guns again, no matter what! He walked over to the fireplace, grabbed the poker and stirred the embers. He added some more firewood, then turned and headed for the stairs and his room to finish his restless night's sleep.

John D. Fie Jr.

CHAPTER 2

The bright sun came shining through the bedroom window, waking up Morgan. He could hear the women laughing downstairs. Sitting up, he looked out the window at the sun's position and saw it was mid-morning. He yawned and stretched. "What a night!" he said.

Marlene was the first to spot him standing in the doorframe of the kitchen.

"Hello there, sleepyhead!" Betty and Helen looked over at him.

"I'm glad to see you're still alive. I was going to come up and wake you in a little while," Betty said.

"I haven't slept that hard in a long time," Morgan replied.

"We all know you've had something weighing on your mind, Morgan," Helen remarked.

Betty noticed Morgan looking out the kitchen window. "The men left before sun-up. Cory said he knew what you want him to get done."

Morgan turned away from the window. "Cory's a good man—a real self-starter."

"You haven't forgotten about today, have you?" Betty asked.

Marlene handed him a cup of coffee.

"No. I haven't. I'm surprised you didn't wake me earlier," he said, smiling.

"Ma always used to tell me never wake someone when they're in a deep sleep. A body will let them know when they've had enough."

Marlene and Helen agreed.

"Here, Morgan," said Marlene. "Sit over here. Your breakfast is ready."

The front door slammed shut, and everyone heard spurs scraping across the hardwood floors.

Betty yelled, "Ben, how many times have I told you about wearing those spurs in the house!"

Ben came into the kitchen. "Sorry li'l missy. Plumb forgot again. Me and Johnny didn't see ol' Morg here and got to wondering if he was feeling poorly is all."

"Have a seat, Ben," said Morgan. "I'm feeling fine. I was tired and just needed some more sleep."

Ben nodded in agreement. "I've been finding it mighty hard to roll out in the morning myself. Sign of the times, I reckon. There ain't no telling what time Johnny will get around to rolling out. He and I talked about it over a checky game one time. We're figgering the mind gets long in the tooth with all the thinkin' it did over the years."

"I'm always wondering what you two old pelicans talk about over there while you're playing your checkers," Marlene said.

"Marlene, I've heard quite a bit what these two talk about over the years. Believe me, you don't want to know!" Betty laughed.

Morgan turned towards Helen. "Do you know anything about the workings on your place over there, Helen?"

Helen shook her head. "Nathan never talked about ranch business with me."

"Do you at least know he if kept some record of headcount on the cattle?"

"If he did, it would be in the den," Helen replied. "The only time I would go in there was to bring him coffee or the brandy bottle, so I wouldn't know where to begin to look."

Morgan looked satisfied with her answer. "How long has it been since the herd has been culled?"

Helen looked confused. "Morgan, those cowboys didn't get paid. The way Nathan treated them, I didn't blame them one bit for moving on. I haven't seen one steer since."

Betty frowned and gave Morgan a stern look. "Morgan, you promised no business today. We're going for a ride and a picnic."

"You're right. I did promise, and I'm sorry. The question just popped into my head, that's all."

"Well, stop with the questions. I'll be fixing that basket pretty shortly, and I'd be obliged if you got the team hitched and get ready to leave yourself. Nothing is going to interrupt this day."

CHAPTER 3

Cory had broken up the crew and sent six riders into the high country to scour the brush, ordering them to drive out any strays. The top brush country wasn't fenced, and cattle up that high could be mixed with the other holdings of the Trails End, so Morgan wanted them all out of there.

Over at the Broken Branch, the men were also scouring the brush for strays. They were starting from the westernmost part of that ranch heading towards the Trails End, while the crew from the Trails End took both the N Bar H and their range. They planned to meet at the most northern part of the Trails End by the mountain springs.

Cory took his crew and worked on finishing the fencing and dividing up the range. Charlie and his chuck wagon would stay with the fencing crew for lunch, and then he'd make his way up to the mountain springs where the brush popping crew were. They would remain there until the job was finished. The same plan was in effect on the Broken Branch. By nightfall, two chuck wagons would be set up waiting for the exhausted, hungry men.

***

Helen had suggested to Betty and Morgan that they take their picnic basket to a spot on their range they called Pine Meadows.

Betty laughed. "I remember that place! We all used to go up there in the summer and swim and have a picnic. My pa and Nathan would do some fishing. Yes. That would be fun! Thank you, Helen, for reminding me."

Marlene, Helen, Ben and Johnny stood on the porch waving goodbye and wishing them a good time. When they were out of earshot, Marlene gave Ben a look.

Ben was confused, so Marlene asked, "Ben, you feel like taking a ride with your rifle?"

"It all depends on what it's for, Miss Marlene."

"Follow behind those two. Make sure they're all right, but stay out of sight."

Ben looked down the lane. "You know something the rest of us don't, Miss Marlene?"

"No. I just feel uncomfortable with the boss and Miss Betty off on their own with no protection."

Helen added, "That's some pretty wild country up there, Ben."

"Pack me a sack lunch, Miss Marlene. I'll go get Whiskey ready," Ben said as he headed towards the barn.

Marlene was smiling as she put some sandwiches in a burlap bag, adding some cookies she'd made the day before.

Ben came out of the barn with his horse in tow and made his way over to his house, where he retrieved his buffalo gun. He walked over to the big house where Marlene waiting for him on the front steps.

"You get any slower, Ben, and I swear you'll start growing moss on your head!" Marlene yelled.

Ben laughed. When he reached out to grab the bag Marlene was holding, she held on to it, pulling Ben closer.

"You be careful out there, you old buzzard, you hear?" she whispered in his ear.

Ben recognized that look on her face. "Well, I'll be. How long you been feeling this way, woman?"

"You never mind that right now. You just come back!"

"Don't go fretting over me, Miss Marlene. I'm too young and ornery to die right now."

Helen overheard them. "Ben, never you mind all that foolish talk! You bring your ornery hide back here in one piece so's Miss Marlene can care for you nice and proper like."

"I'll do just that, ladies!" Ben smiled and mounted Whiskey. Putting three fingers to the bill of his hat, he sank spur, and he and Whiskey were on the move down the lane.

CHAPTER 4

Morgan and Betty were enjoying their ride and taking in the spectacular views.

When they hit the lower range of the N Bar H, Betty pointed to the northeast. "We have to go that way, Morgan."

Morgan wasn't listening. Looking down, he remarked, "Boy, was your pa right! Look at this grass! This is prime cattle country, Betty."

Betty tapped him on his arm. "No business today, Morgan! We're going to enjoy this day, do you hear me?"

He grinned. "Sorry, Betty. I couldn't help myself."

Ben had caught up to them by now and slowed down so they couldn't spot him following them. Everything looked normal. He was wondering why Miss Marlene was so worked up. But once Ben realized where they were heading, he became a little concerned. The Pine Meadow, as the folks called it, was in some pretty wild country. Every wild critter in the area went there to water, and you never knew what would show up.

Ben whispered to Whiskey. "We ain't been up in these parts for some time, huh, ol' fella?"

Whiskey's ears popped up. He knew where he was, and was also on the alert. Ben watched the buggy disappear over the rise in front of them and knew they had arrived at the meadow. Ben rode a little farther, then stayed still and waited.

Morgan pulled up the team down by the water's shoreline.

"There's not a pine tree in sight, Betty!"

"That's right, Morgan. Ma, Pa and Helen named it because it reminded them of home back in the hills."

Morgan looked around. "Seems strange finding a lake up here."

"Oh, this is no ordinary lake, Morgan. This one is spring fed. The real name is Spring Meadow. Now, come help me with this blanket so we can relax."

After the blanket was spread out, Betty opened the basket. "Would you like a sandwich now? Or a drink? I brought along some of Pa's good sipping whiskey."

"I think I'll have some of that sipping whiskey, Betty. It will relax me more, I reckon."

Betty poured him a cup, and he took a sip. "Your pa sure knew how to make some good sipping whiskey, that's for sure."

Betty smiled and sat down next to him with a cup of her own. "Everyone in these parts drank Pa's whiskey. When he passed on, you should have seen the sad faces. It was a sight to behold. Tell me, Morgan. What's on your mind? I can tell something is troubling you."

Morgan looked at Betty, trying to make up his mind whether or not to tell her.

"Come on, Morgan. It can't be that bad."

"Yes, it can. I should have listened to Seth and stayed out of sight."

"Morgan, what on earth are you talking about? Now you have to tell me."

"When we went down to that cattlemen's conference, I think this one fella recognized me. I knew the look on his face. I've seen it too many times in the past. He just kept staring at me! Then, late last night a name came to me—Duke Holcomb. That fella was one of three brothers. They dogged my trail relentlessly for months. If anyone is still interested in finding me, it's them!"

"Have you said anything to Seth about this?"

Morgan shook his head. "I didn't know myself until last night. I suppose I really should tell him, just in case they do slip into town."

"That's why you didn't want to go to that conference, and I insisted you go with me. Now I know why I hear you in your room at night. You must be having some terrible dreams."

"It's not so much dreams, Betty. I just can't sleep."

Betty began rubbing Morgan's shoulders. "That alone could drive you out of your mind."

Just at that moment, Morgan heard something hit the tree he was sitting beside. A few seconds later, he saw a muzzle flash and listened for the report of the rifle.

He quickly shoved Betty out of the way and told her to head for cover. He was making his move to follow her when he felt a burning sensation in his upper right leg. He fell over.

"I'm hit! Stay down, Betty!" Just then, there was another rifle shot, only this time it came from close behind him. *This is just great. Now there's two of them, and my rifle's in the buggy!*

Ben put an end to Morgan's worries, shouting, "Get undercover in those bushes behind you, you dang fool! I'll keep you covered. Now, go!"

Another round crashed into the ground beside Morgan, and Ben fired at the muzzle flash coming from across the lake. Morgan saw riders with their pistols out, riding hard and firing at the men shooting at Morgan and Miss Betty.

Ben yelled out again. "Here come the boys!" He headed over to Morgan.

Betty had come out from behind the bushes and was beside Morgan, trying to stop the bleeding.

"Looks like the boys got them on the run, Morgan. Look up on the ridge in that clearing," Ben said.

Two men were riding hard, dragging a horse with an empty saddle behind them. They were on the rim, and then they disappeared with the Trails End cattlehands right behind them.

Tinker had ridden over. He quickly dismounted and ran to Morgan. He quickly assessed the damage.

"My doctoring bag is in the right-hand side of my saddlebags, Miss Betty. Can you bring it and also bring along that bottle of whiskey, please?"

Morgan looked up at Tinker. "I hope you got a good explanation for having that whiskey with you, Tinker."

"In my line of work, boss, you need to carry one. My job is dangerous, and you never know when you're gonna get hit, cut or end up with a few broken bones. That's all I use it for."

The rest of the men had chased off the bushwhackers and were now pulling up. They looked on as Tinker tried to stop the bleeding.

"Wes, get down to the ranch, grab a fresh horse and fetch back the saw-bones and the sheriff. We'll meet up at the ranch. Now, get going pronto," Tinker said.

"Miss Betty, you got any clean rags? We have to stop this bleeding or at least slow it down."

"All we have is this tablecloth and some napkins, Tinker."

"That'll have to do. Start ripping it up into strips for bandages. Ben, hold down the boss while I pour some of this whiskey on that wound."

He turned towards the rest of the men. "All of you head on back, and drive those strays we gathered over to the mountain springs. I'll join you later."

"We'll take the boss here back to the ranch and wait for the doctor," Ben added.

Roper called out, "What do you want us to do with this dead body we got tied down on the back of this horse? We chased them as far as we dared go, Tinker. We brought this one back with us. Maybe someone in town knows who it is."

Tinker looked over at the horse. "Leave him with us. Wes has gone for the saw-bones and the sheriff. We'll bring him along to the ranch so the sheriff can see him. Now, one of you get on down here and help us get the boss in the buggy. Tell Charlie I'll be late for supper."

"Charlie's not going to like that, Tinker. You know that," Roper said laughingly.

Miss Betty overheard the conversation. She looked up at Roper. "You take charge and do as Tinker said. Now, get moving, boys! You're burning daylight. Don't worry about Morgan. We'll see that he's all right."

Ben was bending over Morgan, giving him some sipping whiskey.

"He's going to have one heck of a headache come morning, li'l missy. But for now, he's feeling no pain."

CHAPTER 5

Wes was riding full out when he slid to a stop in front of the ranch corral and jumped off his horse. Chaps came running out of the barn and took charge of the horse.

Miss Marlene and Miss Helen were entertaining the sheriff on the porch when Miss Marlene saw him. She jumped up, yelling, "What's going on, Wes?"

"The boss has been shot! I got no time to talk about it now, Miss Marlene. I got to ride and fetch the sheriff and the doc!"

Sheriff Farley came to the porch rail. "I'm right here, Wes!"

Wes hurried over and told the sheriff everything he knew.

"Take my horse, Wes," the sheriff said. "He's fresh, and he's a fast runner. When you get to town, get the doctor on his way, then go and tell my deputy to round up a posse and meet me here."

Helen and Marlene looked at one another. "Oh, no! Not Morgan!" Helen said. "Betty must be a mess. She's head over heels for him. We'd best get busy, Marlene. Looks like we got a lot of work to do."

Sheriff Farley was very quiet. Helen asked, "What's on your mind, Seth? You've got that look on your face."

The sheriff was quiet.

"All right, Seth. Out with it. I've known you for a long time, and I know that look. What is it?"

"I don't know if I should say anything."

Her eyebrows raised. "It's about me, isn't it?" She stood with her mouth open, both hands covering her face. "This is about Nathan, isn't it?"

The sheriff's look confirmed her thoughts.

"Seth, I'm not a child. You can tell me whatever it is. Believe me."

Sheriff Farley was still unsure if he should, but looking at both women he could see they weren't going to let it go.

"Ladies, you'd better sit down. What I'm about to tell you may come as a shock. Nathan broke out of prison a month or so ago, along with two other men. Everyone assumed they had left the territory. About a week ago, the Summit bank was robbed by three men. Two of the escaped prisoners were identified from the wanted posters. The third man is unknown as he remained outside the bank as a lookout. I think it may have been Nathan."

"When were you going to tell me all this, Seth?" Miss Helen asked. "This mad man is on the loose once again, and you thought I shouldn't know?"

"Look, Miss Helen. I've been worried out of my mind about you all this time."

Helen held up her hand once again, and Marlene added, "Don't tell us, Seth. Not now."

"Miss Marlene, would you mind excusing us for a little while?" the sheriff asked.

Marlene stood up. "I have work to do. I'll bring you two some refreshments. Helen, would you like some tea?" Helen nodded.

"Coffee for me, Miss Marlene," the sheriff said.

Marlene smiled at him and winked.

Sheriff Farley was embarrassed. *She knows what I'm about to say.*

Once Marlene was in the house, Miss Helen said, "I think I know what you're about to say, Seth, but you don't understand."

"Oh, I think I do understand, Miss Helen, but I have to get this off my mind. It's been driving me crazy. I care about you, and I've been worried almost sick. Look. I'm seriously thinking about retiring and settling down, and I'd like to do that with you by my side."

Helen was caught off-guard. "Seth, how long have you felt this way?"

Marlene was listening behind the door and smiled when she heard the sheriff say, "For years, Miss Helen!"

She turned around, and adding a little skip to her walk she snapped her fingers and began singing once again in the kitchen.

Seth heard her. "Does Miss Marlene always sing in the kitchen?

Helen smiled. "Only when she hears good news, which tells me she was listening."

"What are we going to do about her? She's into everything!"

They both laughed. When they spotted the buggy coming up the lane, Seth got up from his chair and walked over to the steps. He tried to look as official as he could, but it was plain to see he was worried about Morgan. Tinker was the first off the buggy and helped Betty down, while Ben pulled up next to the corral with the spare horse and the dead man.

"How is he?" Seth asked.

"I don't know, Seth. It looks pretty bad," Tinker replied. "We managed to stop the bleeding—for the time being anyway."

Seth looked at Betty. "I have a posse on the way out here—"

"No need for a posse, Sheriff," Ben interrupted as he joined them. "Them varmints rode straight north towards the Yellowstone up into that Injin country. By now, they ought to be scalped or staked out to dry spreadeagle on the Big Horn. If

24

you want to do something, have a look-see at the dead one over there, and see if you know him."

"I'll be there in a minute, Ben. I'm just going to help Tinker with Morgan."

Tinker and the sheriff carried Morgan into the house, and Marlene helped to make him as comfortable as possible in his bed until the doctor showed up. She had a bowl of hot water waiting by the bed, along with strips of clean cloth for bandages. She looked at Morgan's wound and could tell they were going to need a lot more. Sheriff Farley walked back outside and over to the dead man. He grabbed a bunch of his hair and took a look at his face.

"Well? Do you know him, Sheriff?" asked Ben.

"Can't say that I do, Ben. He's new in these parts."

"Figures!"

John D. Fie Jr.

CHAPTER 6

Tinker was upstairs with Miss Betty. He was putting pressure on Morgan's wound, trying to keep the blood loss down to a minimum. It was getting close to suppertime, and Marlene was busy in the kitchen. She knew there were going to be a lot of people to feed this evening and had put on a big pot of stew. She'd already baked a couple of extra loaves of bread. Helen was helping as much as she could, and was now kneading some pie dough.

"Are you going to take the sheriff up on his offer, Helen?" Marlene asked.

"So! You were listening in! Seth thought you were when he heard you singing in here."

Marlene laughed. "Well, are you?"

Helen looked at her seriously. "I don't rightly know. I don't know if I want another man in my life."

Marlene frowned. "You'd be a fool not to say yes, Helen. You heard him just as well as I did—he's been fawning over you for years."

Betty came into the kitchen right then and overheard some of the conversation. "Helen, Marlene's right. You know you won't find a better man than Seth Farley. He's been a mainstay in this community for years."

Helen looked at both of them. "He has a dangerous occupation, and you both know it. I don't think I could deal with wondering every day if he'd come home alive or not."

The women had their backs to the doorway and didn't see Seth standing there, listening. "I told you, Helen. I was thinking of retiring."

Startled, all three women quickly turned around.

"Marlene's not the only one who can listen in on private conversations, ladies."

"Seth, you don't know how to properly ask a lady about marrying up," Marlene said. "That's right, Mr. Sheriff. Whatever happened to the quaint tradition of courting?"

"Miss Marlene, you need to be real quiet about this. I could arrest you as a spy and have you shot at dawn you know," Seth said.

Marlene looked scared. "You wouldn't do that to me, would you, Sheriff?"

Betty playfully slapped Seth's shoulder. "Stop scaring her, Seth."

"Plus, I'm of the mind to hand you a fine for not corralling that crusty old mountain man out there. But I'll forgive you if you fill up my coffee cup," he said as he held it out, smiling.

"Seth Farley, that's a horrible thing to say to Marlene," Helen piped up.

Betty was laughing. "I think I'll leave you three to talk over your problem. I'm going back upstairs to tend to Morgan."

"How is he?" everyone asked at once.

Wes came into the kitchen just as Betty replied, "That Tinker sure knows what he's doing up there. He's nearly stopped the bleeding."

Wes added, "Why, there ain't none better to doctor somebody. We both rode together under General Jeb Stuart during the war. They called on Tinker to do the doctoring every time someone got hit, I'll have you know."

"Thank you for letting me know that, Wes," Betty said.

"I came to tell you there's a bunch of wagons coming up this way, Miss Betty," Wes informed her.

She headed for the front porch, followed by the sheriff, Helen, and Marlene.

Mr. Northrupt was in the lead wagon, followed by a whole host of others.

As they neared the porch, Betty asked, "What's this all about, Mr. Northrupt?"

He pulled to a stop. "We heard what happened, Miss Betty, and we came to show our support. Morgan isn't hurt too badly, is he?"

"We're waiting on the doctor now," she replied.

Mr. Northrupt looked at the sheriff. "Sheriff, you need to get into town. Your deputy is having some problems and requires your assistance."

"Getting a posse together?" the sheriff asked.

"I have no idea, Sheriff. He just asked me to relay the message to you."

Sheriff Farley began looking around for his horse. Spotting Wes, he asked, "Where's my horse, Wes?"

"He's back in town, Sheriff. He was played out when I got to town, so Cal at the livery had me leave him. He gave me that sorrel over there for you to use to get back."

Sheriff Farley found Betty and Helen. He explained he had to leave and headed towards the sorrel. When he was ready, he rode over to Helen.

"Miss Helen, will you at least think it over?"

"I already have, Seth. My answer is yes."

Seth reached down and took her hand. "You just made me a happy man."

CHAPTER 7

Seth reached town just about sunset. Everything looked normal until he got to his office and saw a few men he recognized gathered outside.

"Howdy, fellas. What are you standing out here for?" he asked.

"We heard you needed a posse, Sheriff. When we got here, Ken told us to hang around," one of them said.

Seth was relieved there wasn't a problem, and he told them to go home. One of them asked about Morgan. Seth filled them in and said if he needed them, he'd let them know.

Inside his office, he found Ken sitting behind his desk.

"Seth, I'm glad you're back!" Ken exclaimed.

"Where's Tom? Why aren't you out doing your rounds?"

"We've got a problem. Three riders came in here today with a wanted poster."

Seth frowned. "For who?"

"For Morgan Streeter."

"Go get those men outside—quickly!" Seth knew they hadn't left yet because he could hear them talking.

Ken jumped up and half ran to the door. When everyone was assembled inside, Seth asked Ken to get some badges, then swore them in as deputies. He then told Ken to find the three riders and bring them back to the office with the so-called wanted poster.

Once he had left, Seth unlocked the rifle rack and told everyone to grab a rifle and make sure it was loaded. When everyone was armed, he said, "In a few minutes, Ken will bring back three armed men who are suspected of wanting to ambush Morgan Streeter. When I order them to put their guns on the desk, I want all of you to cock those Winchesters and aim them at the men. Do you understand?"

The men all nodded. He then had them spread out around the office. "Remember, men. These are dangerous criminals. I don't know who they are yet, but I intend to find out."

There was some mumbling among the new deputies. When the door opened and Ken walked in with the three men, the office fell deadly silent.

One of the three men said, "Say, what's going on here?"

"Never mind that," said Seth. "I want all three of you to place your firearms on my desk."

"What for?" asked another of the men.

Seth didn't utter another word. Instead, he pulled his .44 and shot the man in the leg. All the deputies cocked their Winchesters at the same time and pointed them at the men.

"In this town, you'll find that when I tell you to do something, I expect you to do it!" said Seth. "Now, place your weapons on my desk, and please don't make a mistake and try anything funny."

There was no hesitation this time. Seth told Ken to grab the other man's weapon off the floor. Then he asked, "Who has the wanted poster?"

The injured man held it up in the air, and Ken took it from him. Seth looked at the poster and laughed, then spoke to the man lying on the floor. "Offering a false instrument to a law official is ninety days." He looked over at the deputies. "Kevin, take Porter with you and go in the back room and fetch those leg and wrist irons."

Seth looked back down at the man. "You're prisoner number one."

One of the other strangers spoke up. "You can't do this! Who do you think you are?"

Seth was still looking over the wanted poster. He stopped reading and looked at the man, then shot him in the foot. "You'll keep your ambushing mouth shut, prisoner number two."

Some of the newly appointed deputies were stifling their laughter while Ken stood there with his mouth open, shocked. He had never seen Seth act this way before. The third man looked scared out of his mind. He was the one Seth wanted to speak to. Seth pointed his gun in his direction, and the man dropped to the floor, begging him not to shoot.

Seth ordered Ken to put him in the chair next to the desk and cuff him. The scared prisoner continued to beg.

"Now we're getting somewhere," Seth said.

Once the other two prisoners' leg and wrist irons had been attached, Seth had Kevin and Porter escort them to their cells. They were in pain from their wounds and asked for a doctor.

Porter said, "Y'all just don't come into this town ambushing innocent people. I reckon you'll see the doctor come morning. There ain't a dang thing we can do fer ya, stranger."

Seth yelled, "What are you two doing in there?"

Porter responded, "They're asking to see the doc, Sheriff!"

Seth replied loudly and clearly, "Let them bleed to death. Get out here!"

Seth sat behind his desk and stared at the man handcuffed to the chair. "Now, why don't we have a chat. Ken, this man looks as if he could do with a nice hot cup of coffee."

The man kept blubbering, "Sheriff, I didn't want to come with them. They made me do it. Please believe me."

Seth sat back in his chair. He could see the man was young. It could be he had been forced to come along. "Who made you come, and what did they make you do?"

"My brothers made me come. They told me to stand outside the bank while they robbed it, Sheriff. I didn't want to do it. They made me."

"Yes. I can see how they might intimidate you into doing something like that, but the fact remains, young fella, you did it. That makes you as guilty as they as are. Why don't you and I make a little deal—you tell me everything, and when the sheriff of Hadlers Gulch gets here, I'll tell him what you've said. How's that? You know what? I didn't get your name."

"My name's Matthew Holcomb, Sheriff. I'm eighteen," he said.

"Now we're getting somewhere. Matthew, why don't you tell me why you and your brothers ambushed that nice man today?"

Matthew looked surprised. "Sheriff, we didn't ambush anyone. We came here straight after the bank robbery. Percy said with that wanted poster, we could get that fella. After we left town with him, they would do to him what he did to our older brother."

Seth looked surprised. "Which one is Percy?"

"He's the one you shot in the leg. My other brother's name is Ethan. He said we could all take turns killing him. But I don't want to kill no one, Sheriff. I ain't never shot a gun before, and that's the truth."

Seth sat quietly for a while, then instructed Ken to put wrist cuffs and leg irons on the prisoner.

"I believe you, Matthew. You look as if you're telling the truth. So, here's what we're going to do. You're going to remain here under arrest and work around the jail for me until I can make other arrangements."

Seth was confused. *Who had shot Morgan?* The only possibilities he could think of were Matthew's brother, Ethan, or Nathan and the two escaped convicts.

When Ken finished putting on the leg and wrist irons, Seth sent him over to Miss Catherine's Café to order some supper.

"I'm not even going to lock you in a cell, Matthew. You'll sleep in the extra bunk in the back room with me. But if you try to escape, the whole deal is off. Do I have your word?"

Matthew was relieved not to be in a cell. "Yes, Sheriff. I don't want to be no criminal anyhow, Sheriff. My ma always wanted me to get some good book learning and be a good citizen, but Pa made me work and do as he said. It got worse when I had to listen to Percy. I'll do anything you say, Sheriff."

Seth looked at all the new deputies. "Okay. That about finishes things up for today, fellas. I want all of you back here tomorrow morning no later than nine to do some riding. Go on home now, and get some sleep."

CHAPTER 8

Once the doctor arrived at the Trails End, things began to settle down. He was shown directly to Morgan's room where he found Tinker hard at work still trying to keep the bleeding down. He informed the doctor about the slug in Morgan's leg. The doctor cleared the room immediately, but asked Tinker to stay.

Cory arrived back at the ranch headquarters with his crew and was updated. All the men looked shocked. The ranch yard looked as if half the community was there. Tim ran to the house and was stopped by Betty. She took him aside and explained what had happened. It was clear to see he was upset. He stuck by Betty's side and began to cry.

Cory was upset and wanted to speak to the doctor. Marlene took him aside and tried to settle him down.

Finally, after hours of waiting for the doctor and Tinker to make some announcement, they finally made an appearance on the porch. The doctor took Miss Betty aside, while Miss Helen held on to Tim.

Miss Betty then yelled out to everyone. "Can I please have everyone's attention! The doctor will let you know about Morgan's condition."

The doctor raised his hands and called for everyone to come close. "Mr. Streeter, as you all are well aware, received a severe leg wound today. Although serious, it is not life threatening. We've managed to stop the bleeding, but it will take some time to heal. The important thing is that Mr. Streeter is out of danger, folks."

Cheers went up, and everyone started asking questions. The doctor held up his hands once more and asked if the minister would come up and give a prayer of thanks.

Afterwards, Marlene ushered the doctor and Tinker into the house for something to eat and some rest. Marlene felt they both needed it. Betty was crying into Helen's shoulder, shedding tears of joy.

After hearing the good news, Cory settled down the ranch hands. "Let's get something to eat and then hit the bedrolls, fellas. You know the boss wouldn't want it any other way."

After a little bit of socializing with neighbors and friends, even the wagons began to leave. Soon the Trails End returned to normal.

CHAPTER 9

Seth, as usual, was up before dawn and made a pot of coffee. He sat at his desk and started on some paperwork. He'd had one of those nights and hadn't slept well. Too many unanswered questions were running through his mind but first, he needed to find out if anyone had seen Nathan in the area recently. He wondered how the Holcomb brothers knew where to find Morgan and where he'd be on that day. His thoughts were interrupted by the smell of coffee brewing. He got up and poured himself a cup. He had just sat down again when he heard keys in the front door. Tom came in with his cheerful hello.

"I got you your paper, Sheriff!"

Seth Farley greeted Tom in return and asked, "How were your eggs this morning?"

"I didn't have eggs this morning, Seth. Nope. My wife was up early today and made me something called an omelet. It had real fresh cheese in it, and she chopped up some bacon and mixed that in also."

"Did you say fresh cheese?" Seth asked.

"Yeah, Seth. I sure did! We got us a dairy farmer now that knows how to make cheese, and he sold a mess of it to the dry goods place. My wife got it there."

"Tom, I hate to tell you, but you did have eggs this morning. They were just made a different way, that's all. That omelet was made with eggs."

Tom shook his head as he walked into the back room for his morning cup of coffee. Coming back, he asked, "Who's the new visitor, Seth?"

"Oh. That's Matthew. He'll be helping out here for a while. He's a prisoner and bears watching. He's got a few extra privileges that the other prisoners don't have. While I'm on the subject, keep him away from the other two locked up in the cell block. Ken will handle them. He's a good kid who's been raised the wrong way, and we're going to see he stays on the straight and narrow. Understand, Tom?"

Tom nodded. "You know, Sheriff, I've never met someone like you before. Look what you did for me. I think I'm starting to get back in my wife's good graces again. This kid in the back—how many others have there been?"

Seth smiled. "Your wife makes you a special breakfast like that, and you think you're just starting to get back into her good graces? Tom, you've been there for some time now. Make sure you stay there."

Ken entered the office through the back door as always, and greeted Tom and Seth.

"Cal had your horse ready, Seth. He handed him off to me as I passed by. He's in the corral out back with mine. I pitched them some hay to keep them busy for a while."

"Thanks, Ken. I want you to handle those two in the cell block one at a time before letting them out. You have them turn around with their back towards you, and run the length of chain up through their legs. That way if they try anything funny, you just give the chain a good yank. They get no extra anything—only what they need to keep them alive. I want those snakes to suffer like poor Morgan is right now."

"What happened to Morgan?" Tom asked.

"He was on a picnic lunch with Miss Betty yesterday afternoon and was ambushed by these varmints, although Matthew says they didn't do it. One thing's for sure, they robbed a bank down in Hadlers Gulch just the other side of Summit City. They're dangerous, and they're killers. That's why I want Ken to handle them.

"Don't give them an inch, Ken. Not one single inch. Shoot to kill if they try anything—and I mean anything."

"I understand, Seth. I wondered why you did what you did last night. Now I know. Not one inch, and they're to keep their mouths shut."

"Now you got the picture. Tom, I also want those two cell windows boarded back up. They're only to have sunlight for one hour a day. No communication with the outside world. Understand? The men I deputized last night will be going with me today. Also, keep your eyes peeled for any strangers coming into town. Until I discover what's going on, we're locking this town down."

Seth did his early morning rounds and returned to the office, finding his breakfast waiting for him. Matthew was up and eating at the desk, while Tom was sweeping out the jail. The prisoners had eaten, and Ken was out back feeding the horses. So far, it looked as if it would be a normal day.

Once the newly appointed deputies started to arrive, things began to change. Seth had given them various assignments. Two deputies went over to the hotel and cleared out the rooms the prisoners had rented, returning with their belongings. Another went to the livery and notified Cal that the prisoner's horses were now the property of the sheriff's office. Seth told Matthew to take his saddlebags into the back room and empty their contents on the bed, along with everything in his pockets. Seth followed, checking out everything he had, which wasn't much. He then handed Matthew a spare blanket and told him to remove his clothes and wrap himself in it. Calling for Tom, he gave him enough money to get Matthew two sets of clothes. Matthew then threw everything he was wearing into the sack.

"I run a clean jail here, Matthew. When Tom gets back, I'll have him get a tub of hot water ready for you to wash up before you put on those new clothes. You look as though you could use a good haircut, too. We'll see to that later."

Ken was in the outer office vouchering everything. When Seth came back, Ken was holding up two small sacks filled with money.

"What do you want to do with all this money, Seth?"

"That money belongs to the bank in Hadlers Gulch, Ken. It has to be counted and verified by the bank here. I'll have to write out a voucher, get three witnesses to sign it, and then turn it in."

Ken grinned. "Just think of what we could do with all this money, Seth!"

"Get that idea right out of your head, Ken. I'm sure there's a reward for it. We'll probably get a small portion of that."

John D. Fie Jr.

CHAPTER 10

By mid-morning, the sheriff and his posse were pulling up in front of the house on the Trails End. They were greeted by Helen who was sitting outside on the porch reading to Tim. She gave everyone a hearty welcome.

"Howdy, Miss Helen. How's Morgan doing?"

Helen smiled. "He was awake a little while ago, Seth. The doctor and Tinker are still with him upstairs. I think Betty and Marlene are in the kitchen. Go on in."

Seth dismounted and wrapped the reins around the hitching post. "Thanks, Miss Helen. I'll do that."

He climbed the porch steps and stopped to speak with Tim. "How are you getting along, Tim?"

"A whole lot better, Sheriff, now that I know my pa is okay."

"It was a pretty scary thing, wasn't it?"

"It sure was. I thought I was losing another pa."

Seth turned around and told his posse to water the horses while he went inside. He went over to Tim and rubbed the top of his head, tousling his hair. "No need to worry anymore about your pa, okay?"

He walked inside, calling out for Miss Betty, and headed towards the kitchen.

"Howdy, ladies. How's Morgan this morning?"

"Much better, Seth," Betty replied. "The doctor and Tinker worked all night to stop the bleeding. He was awake and alert just a little while ago, then fell back asleep. He's very weak from the loss of all that blood."

Marlene asked, "Sheriff, would you like a cup of coffee?"

"Marlene, I thought you'd never ask!" He placed his hat on the chair by the table and sat down.

"I'm afraid this is both a social and an official visit, Miss Betty. I hope you don't mind if I ask you a few questions?"

"No, Seth. Of course not. Go right ahead."

"What can you tell me about yesterday?"

"Nothing much. Morgan and I were having a picnic lunch out on the Spring Meadow when the first bullet hit the tree by Morgan's head. He shoved me out of the way and told me to get under cover. He was running behind me when the second bullet hit him in the leg. Then we heard another shot from behind us. Suddenly, we heard Ben yelling for Morgan to get under cover. Luckily, our ranch hands were in the area chasing strays out of the brush, and they chased off the bushwackers."

Seth was trying to picture it in his mind. "I've got three brothers over in the jail. They had a phony wanted poster with Morgan's name on it."

"Did you say three brothers?" Betty asked. "Morgan said something yesterday about three brothers, Seth. I can't remember their names, I was so petrified. You'll have to ask him."

"I see. Well, one of them is cooperating and says it wasn't them that did the shooting. But I found out later they had robbed a bank also. I've got two of them in cells, and the youngest is swearing they made him go with them."

Betty looked confused. "You believe him?"

"Yes. I do. But I have to find out where they fit in with Morgan, and if they didn't do it, who did? I suppose you know about Nathan by now?"

Miss Betty nodded. "Do you think it was him, Seth? He was threatening revenge and saying some horrible things."

"Nathan and the two he's with were alleged to have done the bank job. There's been only one bank robbery in the territory by three men, and it wasn't the three of them. The two I have in jail did the bank job, and the younger brother was made to wait outside as a lookout. I have no other choice but to believe it was Nathan and those two murderers he's with."

Betty was wide-eyed. "Surprisingly, Helen thinks so too."

Seth took out his neckerchief and began wiping his forehead. "Could you go up and see if Morgan is awake? I'd like to know why these three are looking for him."

"He said something yesterday about thinking someone had recognized him at the Cattlemen's Conference in Summit City," Betty said.

"You and Morgan went to that conference?" Seth asked, his interest piqued.

"Please don't blame Morgan, Seth. I made him go. He didn't want to."

"It's no wonder people are taking pot shots at him. I told him to lay low, no matter what. All it takes is one person to recognize him. Now I really do need to talk with him. Do you mind if I go upstairs and see if he's awake, Miss Betty?"

"No. Go ahead. But I'm pretty sure he's sleeping."

Seth grabbed his hat and stood up. "Miss Betty, when a man tells you he doesn't want to do something, there's a reason behind it." He turned and headed up the stairs.

Marlene had been starting supper when Seth stomped out. She turned towards Betty. "What was all that about?"

"Oh, Marlene. It's a long story. I'll tell you about it later, okay? Right now, I have a horrible headache worrying about Morgan. I'm going to lie down for a while."

"You go right on ahead, Betty. Get some rest. I can handle what I have to do. I can't believe everything that's going on."

"Don't you worry about it, Marlene. We'll get it all straightened out soon."

A little while later, Seth came back downstairs. He was in a horrible mood.

"Where can I find Ben, Marlene?"

"He's most likely over at the house with Johnny playing checkers."

John D. Fie Jr.

CHAPTER 11

Marlene was standing on the porch having a cup of coffee when she spotted Ben and the sheriff coming out of the house across the way. Ben had his rifle in his hand and was heading for the horses.

"Where are you going, Ben?" Marlene shouted.

"Never you mind where I'm going! You tend to your chores, and I'll tend to mine!"

"Is she trying to set some hooks into you, Ben?" Seth asked, laughing.

Ben frowned. "You can also tend to your chores, and never mind all that laughing."

"My goodness, Ben. Did I hit a sensitive nerve?"

"Are we heading out to that spot you want to see, or are we going to burn daylight sitting here talking about women? I got a checky game to finish and some discussing to do with Johnny," Ben said.

"You're right, Ben. Let's ride!" answered Seth.

Helen had come out onto the porch and joined Marlene at the railing. They watched as Seth, Ben, and the posse left the ranch. Helen looked over at Marlene. "Now, where do you suppose they're going?"

"I don't know, but I got told to tend to my chores, and he'll tend to his."

Helen began laughing. "Now that sounds like Ben talking! I thought I heard him carrying on about something."

The group reached the spot where the shooting had taken place. Ben showed them where Morgan and Betty had been, and then pointed across to the bushes on the other side of the lake.

"That's a pretty long shot to make. Whoever it was must have been using a high powered rifle to make that shot," Seth surmised.

"More than likely he used a buffalo gun, Sheriff," said Ben. "Look at the hole in the tree over here."

They walked over, and the sheriff gave out a soft whistle. "From the height of this hole, I'd say he was aiming for Morgan's head. He would have taken it right off. No, Ben. This was a deliberate shot. Someone wants Morgan dead real bad."

"That's what I'm thinking," answered Ben.

Seth was now looking over at the bush Ben had pointed out to him. "Let's get over to the other side and have us a good look-see around there," he said.

Once they reached the other side of the lake, they spread out. Ben headed over to the bush where he thought the shooter had been hiding and spotted some spent matches on the ground.

He called over to Seth, "He was sitting here waiting and smoking a pipe, I'd say. I don't see any butts laying around, but there's something over here." Ben bent down and picked up an empty cartridge. He was looking it over when Seth joined him.

"He was using a Sharps rifle. Look at this cartridge. It's from a model older than mine with a hefty grain load—a single shot breech loader," Seth said. "But how did they know Morgan would be there having a picnic?"

Ben raised his eyebrows. "That's a good question. I think we got us a rotten apple in the basket, Sheriff."

"But who? Not many knew about them coming out here. A nice lonely spot like this… two people alone having a picnic… can't figure it out yet. This is going to take some hard thinking," Seth said.

"Not hard at all, Sheriff. We're dealing with a polecat. To catch a polecat, you need to set a trap."

"I think you're right, Ben. Let's put our heads together and think for a while on this."

Just then, one of the deputies called out, "Up here! I found the campsite!" Ben and Seth made the climb and joined the deputy.

"The camp's still set up, and it looks as if they were planning to come back to this spot. But why?" Seth pondered.

"I can't figure this one out, Sheriff. It does as if they were coming back here. You don't go and kill someone and then wait around to see what comes next."

The sheriff agreed. "How about to enjoy his kill?"

"You mean this killer has a real grudge, doesn't he?"

"Yes. It's likely he's still hanging around," Seth said.

Ben shook his head. "I saw two riders skedaddle up over that ridge in the clearing over yonder. They were heading straight north. Come on. I'll show you why you won't see him anymore."

Just as they were getting on their horses, another deputy called out, "Sheriff ! Come over here and have a look-see at this!"

The deputy had gone through one of the saddlebags and found a newspaper clipping. The sheriff read it and handed it to Ben.

"There ain't no use handing that to me, Sheriff. I can't read a lick. My pa didn't see no need for us boys to be learning all that book stuff."

"There's only one person who can tell us what this is about, Ben. I can't talk about it right now, but I have a feeling Nathan has nothing to do with this, either."

"What are you talking about Nathan for? He's in prison, isn't he?" Ben asked.

Seth looked surprised. "You mean you didn't know? He broke out of prison with two other convicts."

"No! I had no idea! You're figuring he's headed this way, huh?"

"Yes. I am. But after seeing this newspaper clipping, I'm not so sure it is Nathan. Something else is going on here."

"Well, he'd be a dang fool to come back this way. Just about everyone doesn't want him around here anymore," Ben said.

The sheriff had a faraway look.

"Did you hear me, Sheriff?" Ben asked.

"No, Ben. Sorry. My mind was wandering."

"Stop thinking so much. You'll get your mind all tuckered out and you won't be any dang good to no one. All we have to do is set a trap, and catch the polecat."

"Let's get back to the ranch, and then I'll head into town. I think I've found enough evidence today to think about," Seth said.

"All right. But stop all this thinking. I told you, if you stop thinking about it so much, the answer will pop into your head," Ben said knowingly.

The sheriff called it quits for the day and told the posse they'd be heading back to town. It was getting near suppertime, and they had a fair piece to go.

When they reached the fork in the road, Seth spoke quietly to Ben. "Not a word about what we found out today, you hear? This case is an ongoing investigation, and no one's to know anything about it. Understand?"

"So, you think I'm right about this polecat, huh?"

Seth smiled. "Yes, Ben. I do. I also think it's someone we know and is close to us. I'm going to stay in town tomorrow. Keep your eyes peeled out here, okay?"

"Sure will, Sheriff. You be careful poking around. I'm thinking that polecat was waiting on something—or someone."

"Yes, they were. They knew no one would look for them out in this part of the country. I'm thinking they were waiting to get paid."

"That would mean if it's someone close—like from the ranch—it would have to be someone that goes into town a lot. The only person that comes to mind is Miss Marlene when she delivers her eggs, Sheriff."

CHAPTER 12

Ben pulled up in front of the corral by the barn. Chaps met him and offered to take care of his horse. Betty spotted him heading for the house and called him over.

"What happened out there, Ben?"

"Nothing much, li'l missy. We looked all over out there and found the empty shell casing and their campsite. We know it was a Sharps rifle. Other than that, the sheriff is no further along than he was before." Ben didn't like the idea of having to hold back the truth from her, but the sheriff didn't want anyone knowing what was going on.

"Whoever that dead fella is, he must have wanted Morgan dead real bad. We looked at the bullet hole in the tree, and he was aiming for Morgan's head and missed. I'm thinking we should put some extra men on watch to know who's coming and going—just like your pa did during that Injin ruckus— until this whole thing is over."

Betty thought for a few moments. "I think you may be right. I'll talk to Cory." She turned to go back into the house, and Ben continued on his way to see Johnny and finish that checkers game.

Ben and Johnny were sitting on the porch playing checkers when Cory and the rest of the ranch hands pulled up around sunset. Ben signaled to Cory.

"Howdy, Ben. Something I can do for you?" Cory asked.

"Miss Betty wants to see you." Cory gave Ben the high sign and headed for the house.

CHAPTER 13

Seth and the posse pulled up in front of the livery. He sent the rest of the posse on to the jail to wait for him. Cal came to the door as he was getting off his horse.

"Howdy, Seth. Something I can do for you?"

"Cal, you surprised me. I didn't think you'd be here this late."

Cal gave out a soft chuckle. "Normally, I wouldn't be. I just had a lot of paperwork to deal with. It can get pretty busy around here during the day."

Seth agreed. "Look, Cal. I'm worn out, and so is my horse. Do you think you can get your man to give him a good rubdown and take care of him tonight? I won't be needing him tomorrow, but I will need a fresh mount."

"Don't you worry about a thing, Sheriff. We'll take care of everything."

With that done, Seth walked down the boardwalk, casually greeting some townsfolk. When he was about halfway to his office, he heard his name being called. Looking over in the direction of the voice, he could see both the mayor and the judge standing in the front of the café.

Walking over, Seth asked, "Something I can do for you, Mayor?" He looked at the judge. "Your Honor. You're out late today, sir."

"We're about to get some coffee," said the mayor, "and I overheard Sam talking about fresh apple pie earlier today. Why not join us, and we can have a little chat?"

Seth agreed, and they all entered the café. Seth was hanging up his hat when he noticed a stranger sitting at a corner table facing the door. He instantly pegged him for being either a gunhand or an owl-hoot. He walked over and introduced himself.

"Howdy, stranger. New in these parts, ain't ya?" Seth was standing hipshot with the heel of his right hand over the butt of his holstered .44 and his left thumb hooked to his gun belt. He could see the stranger was trying hard to avoid eye contact and kept his head down while he ate.

"I got in about an hour ago. Why?"

"Why? Interesting question. Because it's my job to know, that's why. Now, stand up and keep those hands in full sight."

The judge and the mayor were standing by a table when the mayor called out, "What's this all about, Sheriff?"

Seth could hear the judge say, "Leave him be, Harold. He's doing his job."

"Now, with two fingers on your left hand, gently reach across and pull that hog leg out of the holster, and lay it gently down on the table. Do it real slow like, Mr. ..."

Out of the corner of his eye, Seth caught sight of Ken easing in through the back door with his gun out. When he was in position, Ken said, "I'm right here, Sheriff."

"I know you are, Ken. I can see you out of the corner of my eye. Now, come around the counter and escort our friend here down to the jail and lock him up."

Annoyed, the stranger asked, "On what charge?"

"There is no charge yet. I'm holding you for questioning."

Ken was now behind the stranger and poked him in the back with his gun. "Get moving!"

"I'll be there in a little while, Ken. Put him in number one."

"All right, Sheriff."

By this time, the mayor and the judge were sitting down. Seth joined them.

The mayor frowned. "What was that all about, Sheriff?"

"We're going to have to bring back a few town ordinances until this investigation is over, I'm afraid. Would that be hard to do?"

"No. We just have to have the town council in agreement and take a vote. I must say though, with the way business is going these days, it might prove difficult to pass a vote. Why can't you just add more deputies?"

"I could do that, but I don't want to upset the apple cart and hurt business. Right now, we have a situation where I need to know who's coming and going in and out of town."

"Why don't you try adding deputies first, Sheriff. We still have that special fund set up in case we need more," the mayor said.

Seth nodded. Sam came over to take their orders of coffee and pie.

"Mayor, you're also president of the bank. If it is who I think it is, and he swore revenge on anyone that had done him wrong, you could also be in danger. I'm apprehensive about this whole situation, and I don't want to see anyone get hurt. I might be forced to gun him down like a mad dog. That might not make me very popular around these parts."

"I don't think you need to worry on that score, Sheriff," the mayor replied.

"I have something else to discuss with you, Your Honor, but I think it can wait another week or two."

The judge smiled. "Anytime, Sheriff. You know that. Just come down to my chambers at the courthouse. I'm more than happy to help you out."

Seth finished his coffee and pie. He was reaching into his pocket for some money when he heard the mayor say, "No need for that, Sheriff. It's my treat. Besides, I'm curious. I suppose you're headed for your office now to question that stranger. What made you walk over to him like that?"

Seth let out a soft laugh. "The way he was seated, and the way he was acting when we walked in. By not looking at me, he was trying hard not to make eye contact, and he was answering a question with a question. He's either a gunhand or an owl-hoot on the scout. I'm going to find out which one."

CHAPTER 14

Morgan opened his eyes and looked around. At first, he didn't know where he was. Looking down at his chest, he saw Betty sound asleep, and his memory slowly came back. He spoke softly to her. When she woke up and realized he was awake, she began kissing him and crying tears of joy. Morgan was still in a bit of shock and asked, "How long have I been out of it?"

"Just about two weeks now, Morgan. We were all worried about you!"

He looked confused. "I don't remember what happened. Was Ben there?"

Betty grabbed a damp cloth from the side table and wiped his forehead.

"Take it easy, Morgan. You're all right, and that's the main thing. You had a bad fever, and it had us all worried."

Marlene heard them talking and came into the room.

"Mr. Morgan! You've come back to us!"

"Yes. For now, Marlene. But if you start singing, I'm going right back where I was."

Betty and Marlene started laughing. "Morgan, that's a horrible thing to say to Marlene," Betty commented.

"After all the worrying I've been doing over you, this is the way you treat me?" Marlene said.

Morgan laughed.

"You can stop your fussing over him now, Betty. He's all right and back to his old self, too. Are you hungry? Do you want something to eat, Mr. Morgan?" Marlene asked.

"Remember what the doctor said about when he wakes up, Marlene," said Betty.

"Yes. I've had a pot of soup on every day just in case he woke up, along with some fresh bread. I'll bring some up right away."

"Water! I'm thirsty!" Morgan said.

Betty calmed him down. "I've got some water right over here for you in the pitcher." She brought him a cup of water and helped him drink it.

While he had the cup up to his mouth, she said, "The doctor said you'd need to build your strength back slowly. You lost a terrible amount of blood, and it's going to take time for you to get up and do what you did before. For the next few weeks, you're going to remain right where you are. I don't want to hear one argument out of you. Do you understand?"

Morgan began to protest. "I can't just lie here, Betty. I've got a ranch to run, and I can't run it from here."

Betty placed a couple of fingers over Morgan's lips. "The ranch is running just fine, Morgan Streeter. Now, you stay here and rest."

Morgan put his head on the pillow and was out like a light in no time. Betty heard Marlene climbing the stairs and went to tell her that Morgan had fallen back to sleep.

CHAPTER 15

Seth was sitting behind his desk, filling out paperwork. He had been notified that the territorial prison wagon was on its way to pick up the Holcomb brothers and transport them back to stand trial for bank robbery and murder. *It will be good to get those troublemakers out of my jail.*

Just then, Ken opened the door and escorted three men into the office, all wearing stars on their shirts.

"Hello, Sheriff. I'm Deputy Grassley. These gentlemen are Deputies Frank and Cullem. We're here to transport the Holcomb brothers. I was told to give you this." The deputy handed a package to the sheriff.

Seth nodded. "Thank you. Deputies, your prisoners are in the back cell block. Ken, will you take them please?"

Ken stood by the cell block door, allowing the deputies access to the prisoners.

Seth opened up the package, finding yet more forms to fill out. He got back to work, finishing the paperwork and signing the voucher for the ten thousand dollar reward. *Ten thousand dollars split nine ways makes a great pay for the month. I'm sure next time a call goes out for a posse, I won't be short of men.*

Ken came back into the office with the two prisoners behind him, shackled to one another.

"Is this all they have? No boots or other clothes?" Deputy Grassley asked.

Sheriff Farley looked at the prisoners for the first time since the day they were arrested. "That's it, Deputy. Their clothing had to be burned, along with their boots and hats. It's all here in my paperwork—everything they had."

"Just as well," the deputy replied. "Where these two are going they won't be needing any clothing. The long-handles will do just fine."

One of the brothers started to say something and got rewarded with a rifle butt between the shoulder blades that sent him to his knees. The deputy directly behind him pulled on his neck chain, and the prisoner began gasping for air as his hands shot up towards his throat.

Deputy Grassley kicked him in the stomach. "No one told you to add your two cents' worth. Shut up, or next time it will be your jaw that gets the rifle butt."

"I dislike prisoners with bad manners, Sheriff," the deputy explained.

"As do I, Deputy," Seth replied.

The prisoners were then escorted out of the jailhouse and into the wagon where they were chained to the floor. Deputy Grassley got on his horse.

He turned towards the sheriff and his deputies. "Pleasure doing business with you folks." He turned his horse's head, and off they rode.

Seth turned to Tom. "Go down to the livery, and tell Cal to get that horse ready for that fella we're holding in there. We're cutting him loose."

Tom headed off as Seth watched him limp down the boardwalk. He smiled and went back into his office. Ken followed and waited while the sheriff sat down behind his desk, opened up his top drawer, and pulled out some papers.

"Ken, go in the cell block and bring out that prisoner fella. We're cutting him loose. There's no wanted poster for him and no record of anything, so he goes free."

Ken headed to the cell block. When he brought the prisoner back, he pointed over towards the desk, then released the wrist cuffs.

Seth looked at the prisoner. "Why do you look confused?

"I wondering what I'm doing here like this, Sheriff," he said.

Seth was short and to the point. "I'm letting you go. There's no wanted poster for you, and it looks as if no one has ever heard of you. I have no other alternative but to turn you loose with a warning, Don't step foot in this town ever again, or I'll arrest you. Now, which way are you heading?"

The prisoner scratched his head. "I was heading west out to Calfornia, Sheriff."

"If I were you, I'd head south, not north. There's word that something's stirred up the Indians north of here. So, if you like your hair on your head, head south. Okay. Sign this paper, and read this one," the sheriff said as he pushed some paper across his desk.

"Ken, as soon as he signs these, walk him down to the livery and take him out to the town line, then get back here. We've got more work to do on the shooting out on Spring Meadow.

"I'm a bit hungry. I think I'll go over to the café for something to eat and meet you back here." The sheriff walked over to the hat rack, put on his hat and looked back at the prisoner once more.

"You remember what I told you, young fella. Don't come back."

CHAPTER 16

Tom arrived at work bright and early with a smile on his face, eager to start his new job. Seth had given Tom a raise in pay and a desk of his own to do filing and paperwork, while young Matthew was now the office boy and cleaner.

Tom walked over to the sheriff's desk. "I got the morning paper here for you, Sheriff."

Seth was eating breakfast. "What's got you so bright and chipper this morning, Tom?"

Tom was smiling from ear to ear. "My wife made me another one of those special breakfasts again this morning. She told me how proud she was of me sticking to my word and staying away from the whiskey. We even have a bank account again, and she's happy we have a line of credit at the dry goods store again. Barney told her over at the mercantile how proud everyone is, and folks are happy to see me. It's all thanks to you, Sheriff."

Seth was just as happy for Tom. "Tom, I had nothing to do with it. You were the one that made an effort after seeing how drinking was affecting your marriage. Plus, finding your wife that way in that snowstorm... No, Tom. The credit belongs to you."

Tom sat behind his desk, smiling. Ken came through the back door and said good morning to everyone, and the sheriff gave him his orders for the day.

"Ken, when the rest of the men get here, I'm taking five of them with me to look over the spot where Morgan got shot. I just have this nagging feeling there was something I missed."

"Like what, Seth?" asked Ken. "It's been pretty near a month already."

Seth knew Ken was right. By this time, most of the tracks would have disappeared, but Seth still had this nagging feeling he had missed something. He still hadn't had a chance to talk to Morgan about that day. He was going to stop by the Trails End to check on him and see Ben.

"I know you're right, Ken, but that day we were all in shock that someone had tried to kill Morgan. The signs all pointed to Nathan. What's strange about this whole thing is that there still haven't been any sightings of Nathan and those other two that escaped with him. This whole affair just keeps nagging at me."

The rest of the deputies showed up at the same time and entered the sheriff's office. Ken spoke while Seth put on his gun belt and hat.

"Porter, you stay in town today with me. The rest of you are heading back out to the spot where Morgan got shot to have another look around. The sheriff wants to talk with Morgan. Maybe he's awake now, and the sheriff can get a little more information."

Seth was soon ready to go. "Ken, tell Matthew to strip down those bunks today in the cell block and air out the blankets. Also, take down those shutters on the cell windows, and then run the dirty laundry down to the Chinese wash to have them boiled clean."

With that, Seth left the jailhouse with his five men and headed for the Trails End.

John D. Fie Jr.

CHAPTER 17

The women were sitting on the porch talking when Cory walked up.

"Is the boss up yet this morning, Miss Betty?"

"Yes, he is, Cory. He's having his breakfast. Why don't you go on in and cheer him up a little. He'll be happy to see you."

Cory pulled off his hat. "Thank you very much, Miss Betty. I won't be long."

"Take as long as you like, Cory. You haven't seen him in a while."

Cory bounded inside and took off up the stairs.

When he was out of earshot, Betty said, "That Cory is so nervous around me. How do you settle someone like him down?"

"Most cowhands are shy around women, Betty. Haven't you ever noticed that before? All they know is cattle and horses. It's the world they live in. They're only used to interacting with other cowboys. They have no idea how to deal with women socially," Helen responded.

Marlene was laughing. "I've noticed that I get that old pelican going all the time."

"You be careful around ol' Ben, Marlene. He's not a cowhand. That old man is a mountain man, and he's wiser than you think," Helen warned.

Just then, Marlene pointed down the lane. "Speaking of men, Helen, here comes yours right now."

"I wonder what brings him out here this time of day," Helen mused.

"I'll bet he's wanting to speak with Morgan. He hasn't spoken to him about the shooting yet. You know Seth Farley. He won't be satisfied until he gets everyone's input."

Seth pulled up to the porch and gave everyone a hearty hello.

"Seth Farley, this has to be official business. You don't normally get out this way until later in the day," Betty said.

Seth dismounted. "Somewhat, Miss Betty." He pulled off his hat and greeted the other ladies.

"I'm missing a few pieces of the puzzle in this shooting."

Betty looked over at Helen, and they both smiled.

Helen spoke up. "Seth, take a break and join us on the porch here. Tell us what's on your mind."

He climbed the steps while Betty stood up and told the posse to take the horses over and water them.

She sat back down. "Okay, Seth. What's on your mind?"

He was silent for a few moments. "Did anyone know you and Morgan were going out for a picnic lunch that day?"

Betty shook her head. "We spoke briefly about it the day before, but no decision was made. Why?"

"To my way of thinking, somehow word of this got out to the shooter, and he was there waiting in ambush. Marlene, think hard. Did you deliver any eggs in town that day and could you have talked with anyone?"

Marlene tried to remember. "I had an egg delivery for the café and the bakery that day, I think. Plus, another emergency order at the hotel. When I finished, I stopped in at the café and had a coffee with Catherine. We sat and talked. She's always asking about Betty and Helen, so there's nothing unusual about that."

She paused. "We did talk about the picnic!" Her hands shot up to her mouth. "Catherine asked me if Betty had won the war yet with Morgan, trying to get him to take off a day."

Marlene turned her head towards Betty. "Betty, I'm so sorry! I didn't know!"

Betty shook her head. "It was a friendly conversation, and you had no idea something like this was going to happen. It could have been any one of us talking with one another like we do. Don't blame yourself."

Seth urged her to continue.

"I absentmindedly mentioned Pine Meadow—that they might go there."

Helen added, "There's only one other person who knows we call it Pine Meadow, and that's Nathan! I didn't want to believe he would do such a thing, but I guess I was wrong."

"Helen, we don't know for sure if it was Nathan or not," said Seth.

He turned his attention back to Marlene. "This is very important. I want to you to sit back and concentrate."

Marlene nodded.

"Was there anyone else in the café at the time you two were talking?"

Marlene thought hard. "Yes! A man was sitting at a corner table. He was wearing a black suit with a black hat on his head, and he was reading a newspaper."

Seth slapped his knee. "Betty, is Morgan awake?"

"Yes. Go on up. Cory's with him."

Seth excused himself and went up to Morgan's bedroom. He stuck his head in the door. "Well, look who's alive!"

Morgan was surprised to see Seth and waved him in.

"To what do I owe this pleasure, Seth?"

The sheriff shoook hands with Cory. "Morgan, can we speak privately for a moment?"

"Sure. Cory, will you excuse us?"

"Sure, boss. Is it all right if the boys come and see you later?"

"Yes, Cory. After supper this evening, send them around."

When Cory came outside, Betty asked, "What was the big conference about, Cory?"

"The boys are wanting to see the boss and wish him well. It's important to them, Miss Betty."

"I don't see any problem with that. Send them around. They're welcome to talk to Morgan anytime. Make sure they know that."

Upstairs, Morgan and Seth were deep in conversation. Seth filled him in about the Holcomb brothers and how he had kept Matthew from joining his brothers at the gallows. Morgan listened intently.

"Morgan, when I tell you to stay out of sight, I tell you that for a reason. These people are out to kill you, and they're not going to come at you in a face-to-face gunfight. You're going to get it in the back. Now, please do as I tell you," Seth pleaded.

"I didn't want to go to that cattlemen's conference in the first place, Seth, but Betty was adamant about going," Morgan said. "To keep the peace, I relented. I won't do that again."

"What does the doc say about that leg?" Seth asked.

"He wants me to stay off it for a while longer. The wound still hasn't completely healed."

Seth was silent for a long while.

"What's going on, Seth? Is there more bad news?" Morgan asked.

"I think you have a bigger problem on your hands now, Morgan. This one is dogging your trail hard, and if it's who I think it is, he's a stone-cold killer. Morgan, you've got to stay out of sight—and I mean entirely out of sight. I hate to say this, but I would recommend hiring a few good men who are good shots for your protection. You have to listen to me. He was waiting for you to show up out there. Somehow he found out where you'd be and took full advantage of it. This man is a hitman with a grudge, and he means business."

Morgan was quiet. "Well, I don't think we need to worry much for a while. With my leg like this, I won't be going anywhere for at least a good month or so."

"You don't know how close you came to not being here, Morgan. You got lucky when he missed your head and hit the tree. According to Ben, he was using one of those old Sharps rifles. We found the empty cartridges. You're a lucky fella."

Seth stood up and put on his hat. "Morgan, you ever hear of a man named Daniel Curley?"

Morgan looked up quickly, and the expression on his face confirmed he had. "Yes, I have. And yes, he has a grudge against me. Why?"

"Because if I'm right, he's the one dogging your trail," Seth answered.

"Can't be, Seth. He's been dead for several years now. At least that's what I heard. He's the one they say raped and killed my wife, then burned down my ranch to get rid of any evidence. I'd been hunting that snake for years."

"He goes by the name Gordon Stiller now. He's a known bounty hunter and also hunts Injin scalps. I had him in my jail a month ago, at least I think it was him.

"I'm going to see if Ben wants to come along. I'm taking a ride up to the meadow to have another look around."

"So, from what I understand, you think he already knew I was here," Morgan mused. "Someone in town must have known all along who I was and sent for him. The Holcombs being here was an accident. And it's all because I made a stupid mistake of going to that cattlemen's conference. My question is, who in town knows who I am?"

"That's what I want to know, too," Seth replied.

"Whoever it is, Seth, they sure have a mighty big thing for me, and they're disguising it pretty well. It's not going to be easy flushing them out."

Seth nodded in agreement. "Well, I'm not going to get to the bottom of this standing here flapping my jaw with you. Just stay out of sight!"

With that, he left the room. When he came outside, the women were still sitting on the porch.

"Did you have a good visit, Seth?" asked Betty.

"It was not only a good visit, Miss Betty, but a mighty educational one at that."

"Are you still coming out to have lunch with us on Saturday?" asked Helen.

"Wouldn't miss it for the world, Miss Helen," Seth said, smiling.

Ben came up just then. "Howdy, you old law dog. You looking for me?"

"Yeah, you broke down old mountain coot." Both men laughed.

"Feel like taking a ride with us, Ben?" Seth asked.

"Whiskey is ready to go. I'll just fetch my rifle."

The posse was already mounted when Ben returned. He headed for the corral and mounted up.

"Lead the way. Let's ride!"

"We're going back to where Morgan got shot, Ben. Do you know another way to get there?" Seth asked.

Ben pointed and then put spur to Whiskey, yelling, "Just follow me, gents!"

The three women watched as they rode off. "It looks like they're heading back out to the meadow," Betty commented.

"What do you suppose he's looking for now?" Helen wondered.

"We all know how Seth is. He's not going to be satisfied until he has all the answerss to the questions in his head. Whatever it is, I hope he finds it," Betty replied.

John D. Fie Jr.

CHAPTER 18

They rode along in silence. After a while, Seth spoke up. "Who's range is this anyway?"

"Right now, it belongs to the Trails End," Ben said, "but it used to belong to that Nathan fella. Real good grass out here for cattle."

Seth looked around. "You're right. But where are all the cattle? I don't see any. Now that I think about it, the last time we were out here, I didn't see any then, either."

"This ranch used to run over a thousand head years back, just like the Trails End. Over the years, while li'l missy's pa kept growing bigger, old Nathan kept getting more ornery and couldn't keep any help. Old man Delaney saw the answer to that. He cut off his supply of sipping whiskey. One thing led to another, and before you knew it, they were feuding."

"So, to pay off his drinking and gambling debts, he would pay them off with a steer or two," the sheriff said.

"Now you got the picture. It's like putting on a pair of them seeing specs, ain't it?"

"Yes, Ben. It's a whole new picture book."

"But that ain't the only aching tooth in this area, Sheriff. I'm gonna tell you one more thing, and then I'm gonna shut my mouth. Do you know who gets paid the most?"

Seth's head snapped towards Ben. "What are you talking about?"

"I talking about that snake in the grass all you folks keep electing as mayor, that's who."

The sheriff saw the other men were busy talking to one another. "Ben, I think maybe we should talk about this another time when we're alone. I have a powerful feeling you're going to tell me something I know I need to hear, and others don't. At least not yet."

"Your assumption would be right, but don't take too long. I got me a nagging ache that says getting rid of Morgan is just the start," Ben added.

The conversation ended as they arrived at the meadow. Seth had the posse spread out and start looking around for any evidence. The search continued for the next few hours until the sun was sitting high in the sky. Seth ordered everyone to take a break and rest for a while. He sat silently thinking while the posse made a cookfire and chatted about their farms and crops while they ate and drank. Ben was resting with his hat over his eyes.

Seth interrupted his sleep. "You know this neck of the woods pretty good, don't you, Ben?"

"Yep. Been around these parts before any white man stepped foot in it."

"Is there anywhere else up here that someone could use as a hideout?"

Ben sat up quickly. "I don't know why I didn't think of it before, but there are several places! There's li'l missy's pa's old still, an old mining shack down the other side of the switchback, and Nathan's old hunting camp up that mountain over yonder east of here."

"After we're finished eating, let's head up to that hunting camp. I want to have a good look around."

When the break was over, and everyone, as well as the horses, were rested, the posse got on their way. It didn't take very long for Ben to find tracks.

Turning, he pointed them out. "Look there, Sheriff. Fresh tracks. Someone's been this way recently."

"How much farther is this hunting camp, Ben?"

"About halfway up. There's a spot around this corner where we can leave the horses and walk up the rest of the way, but I suggest we do it quietly."

Reaching the spot Ben was referring to, the posse dismounted. Armed with their rifles and spare ammunition, they continued on foot. They were nearing the site of the hunting camp when Ben stopped and sniffed the air.

"There's something dead up there, Seth. I'm gonna sneak up and have a look."

The sheriff nodded in approval and Ben set off alone. A little while later, he returned.

"We're alone. Whoever it was, they're gone now. Horse apples are laying around up there all dried up, so it's been a few weeks since anyone was here. The odor is stronger up there. I hope everyone has a strong stomach. This might not be pretty."

The posse broke their climb and made it to level ground, Ben and Seth went straight for the cabin while the rest of the posse searched the area.

Ben kicked in the cabin door. "Well, looky here, Sheriff. As I live and breathe, here's old Nathan with a bullet hole between his eyes."

"Close it up, Ben," said the sheriff. "We're heading back to town."

CHAPTER 19

When the posse reached the meadow once again, everyone was happy to breathe the fresh air. The sheriff held them up and told them to take a break.

Seth looked over at Ben. "We're going to head back to town using the road. From here, it's shorter than going back out to the Trails End. It's easier for you to cut across the way we came this morning. But don't say a word to anyone about what we found. Okay?"

Ben nodded. "I'll just water up Whiskey and go. No need to worry about me, Sheriff. My lips are sealed. I want to see you get these owl-hoots."

"We'll meet up here at daybreak or shortly after, and have a look at those other spots you mentioned."

"I was going to suggest you bring along a packhorse with some supplies, and we could stay out until we find something," Ben suggested.

After Whiskey had had some water, Ben headed back to the Trails End. The sheriff watched until he disappeared over the horizon and then mounted up his posse and headed into town.

When Ben reached the ranch, he knew everyone would be looking for him, so he slowed his pace so he would arrive while everyone was eating supper.

He slipped into the Trails End after dark and met Chaps at the barn door. Placing a finger to his lips, he told Chaps he'd give him a silver dollar for his silence. Chaps smiled and took his horse.

Seth and the posse made it back to town after dark and dispersed with their orders for the morning. Meanwhile, the sheriff sent Ken to get the posse supplies.

CHAPTER 20

Ben arrived first at the meadow and made himself a small fire and some coffee. The day was just beginning when he spotted riders heading his way. It was the posse. He sat back and greeted them as they pulled up.

"Didn't expect you to show for at least another hour, Sheriff."

"Couldn't sleep a wink last night. The rest of these guys get up at this hour every day, Ben."

"Well, I sure don't have any complaints about that. They're a good bunch."

Seth nodded in agreement. "Three of them are ex-military— all cavalry. They ride hard, and fight just as hard."

"That's what I like to hear. You have a posse like this every time, and you can count me in as your tracker."

Seth knew Ben meant business. "Why do you want to do that, Ben?"

"Well, I reckon I've taken a liking to you. There ain't that many law dawgs around quite like you, Sheriff. I knew what you were doing the day you brought Morgan out to the ranch, and I also knew right away what Morgan was by the way he walked and looked at a fella. He has it in his eyes, Sheriff.

That's one of the reasons I moved down to the ranch. I'll explain it all to you when we have that pow-wow."

By this time, the sun was coming over the horizon. "Let's finish up those coffees, men," Seth said. "The sun's up, and we can see where we're going."

A half hour later, the posse was on the trail with Ben in the lead.

Once they reached the mountains, Ben told them to follow him single file and not to wander off the trail. Seth had a few questions, but thought it best to keep them to himself.

It seemed they'd been climbing half the morning. Every once in a while, Ben would stop and have a listen. They arrived at a place where Ben suggested they leave the horses. It was a table top that had plenty of grass for grazing. They continued on foot.

A short while later, Ben stopped and gathered everyone around. Speaking softly, he said, "From here on out, be very careful where you step. If anyone is down in the canyon ahead, they'll hear a rock rolling down the mountian. The air is thin up here, and sound travels, so be as quiet as a church mouse."

Ben started off again, but didn't go far before stopping once again. "I'm going to edge forward and have a peek down into the canyon."

Everyone watched. Once Ben neared the center of the clearing, he lay flat and crawled towards the edge. It didn't take long before he was back.

"Okay. There are at least four men down there. From where we'll be, they'll be bottled up in that canyon. They'll have to come by us to get out. Their horses aren't saddled, so if we miss anyone on our first volley of fire, keep shooting. Sheriff, I don't reckon you want any of those varmints alive, do you?"

Seth shook his head. "Doesn't matter, Ben, as long as we get them."

"How do they say it in the army?" Ben asked, "Oh yeah, I know. When you get to the edge, fan out and form a firing line, men."

"You just had to say that, didn't you?" Seth said.

Ben smiled. "Yep. Just wanted to make the boys feel right at home, that's all."

Ben led, and one by one, everyone followed. Once they were in line, Ben gave a hand signal for them to open up after he fired.

The sheriff pointed out the one in the black suit to Ben. He would take the one in the grey hat. Ben sighted in with the Sharps and fired. The round hit the black-suited man, lifting him up and off the rock he was sitting on, throwing him a couple of feet flat on his back. Seth hit his target, and all hell broke loose. It didn't take long before all was quiet below. Ben stood up and looked down, seeing no movement.

Ben led the posse back to where the horses were tied and then showed them the way down. When they entered the canyon mouth, the posse dismounted and surveyed the damage.

There was no doubt about it. They were all dead. They loaded the bodies on their horses, tied them down and headed for home.

When they reached the meadow, they stopped for a rest.

"You coming along to the ranch or heading for home?" Ben asked.

"I think this posse's earned a taste of pa's sipping whiskey, don't you, Ben?"

"Now I know why I took a liking to you, Sheriff!"

CHAPTER 21

Everyone was in the ranch yard when the posse came riding in and began waving. Charlie rang the chow triangle. Marlene came running out of the house, along with Helen and Betty. Even Old Johnny was standing on his porch steps.

As the posse got closer, Ben remarked, "Well, will you look at that! A welcoming party!"

"It looks like they got them," Betty said. "Seth never gives up!"

Marlene ran to Ben. Reaching up, she grabbed his hand. "Don't you ever leave again without saying goodbye, you old buzzard!"

"Yeah, Ben. What's wrong with you, leaving your intended like that?" Seth teased.

Ben frowned. "What's so funny? Yours is on her way. Keep it up, law dawg, and I may start not liking you again!"

Helen came up to Seth. "I was scared, Seth. Promise me you'll retire."

Betty called for Cory to go to the root cellar for two jugs of sipping whiskey.

The doctor was with Morgan when they heard the commotion outside. "Doc, go see what all the ruckus is about," Morgan said.

"Looks like the sheriff is back with four over the saddle," the doctor replied as he looked out the window.

Morgan breathed a sigh of relief. Whispering to himself, he said, "Looks like it's over."

Just then, Betty burst through the bedroom door with two cups in her hands. "The sheriff is back with Ben and the posse. Morgan, it's over!"

"What's over?" the doc asked.

"Never mind, Doctor. You wouldn't understand. Just enjoy the refreshment. You, above all, deserve it."

Everyone joined them in the bedroom, holding their cups and laughing with joy.

"Hey, bossman," Ben said, "when are you going to get good and tired of lying around and roll out from under that bedroll?"

"You never mind all that, Ben. We're having enough trouble as it is trying to keep him in bed!" Betty replied.

Betty took Morgan's hand and told him about Nathan. Morgan looked worried.

"How is Helen taking it, Betty?"

"Fine, I guess. She was kissing Seth when I left them."

"Maybe we'll have some peace and quiet out here on the Trails End after all."

THE END

A NOTE FROM THE AUTHOR

Well, friends, I hope you enjoyed this edition of the Gunfighter Series and are looking forward to the next installment to the series, which will be along soon. I know you're as excited as I am to once again join Morgan, Betty and the rest of the cast of characters in the next edition to the Gunfighter series in Book 4, Rustlers on the Range.

Made in the USA
Columbia, SC
31 May 2019